THE
LIVES OF ANIMALS

J.M. Coetzee was born in Cape Town, South Africa, and educated in South Africa and the United States. He is the author of eight other works of fiction, two of which, *Life and Times of Michael K* (1983) and *Disgrace* (1999), have won the Booker Prize. Among the other awards his novels have received are the CNA Prize, the premier South African literary award (twice), the Prix Etranger Fémina and the *Irish Times* International Fiction Award.

ALSO BY J.M. COETZEE

Fiction

Dusklands
In the Heart of the Country
Waiting for the Barbarians
Life and Times of Michael K
Foe
Age of Iron
The Master of Petersburg
Disgrace

Non-Fiction

White Writing
Doubling the Point: Essays and Interviews
Giving Offence
Boyhood: Scenes from Provincial Life

THE
LIVES OF
ANIMALS

J. M. COETZEE

P
PROFILE BOOKS

This paperback edition first published in 2000 by
Profile Books Ltd
58A Hatton Garden
London ECIN 8LX
www.profilebooks.co.uk

First published in Great Britain by
Princeton University Press in 1999
Copyright © Princeton University Press 1999

Typeset in Fournier by MacGuru
info@macguru.org.uk

Printed and bound in Great Britain by
St Edmundsbury Press, Bury St Edmunds

A CIP catalogue record for this book is available from
the British Library.

ISBN 1 86197 237 7

CONTENTS

THE
PHILOSOPHERS AND
THE ANIMALS

He is waiting at the gate when her flight comes in. Two years have passed since he last saw his mother; despite himself, he is shocked at how she has aged. Her hair, which had had streaks of gray in it, is now entirely white; her shoulders stoop; her flesh has grown flabby.

They have never been a demonstrative family. A hug, a few murmured words, and the business of greeting is done. In silence they follow the flow of travelers to the baggage hall, pick up her suitcase, and set off on the ninety-minute drive.

"A long flight," he remarks. "You must be exhausted."

"Ready to sleep," she says; and indeed, en route, she falls asleep briefly, her head slumped against the window.

At six o'clock, as it is growing dark, they pull up in front of his home in suburban Waltham. His wife Norma and the children appear on the porch. In a show of affection that must cost her a great deal, Norma holds her arms out wide and says, "Elizabeth!" The two women embrace; then the children, in their well-brought-up though more subdued fashion, follow suit.

Elizabeth Costello the novelist will be staying with them for the three days of her visit to Appleton College. It is not a period he is looking forward to. His wife and his mother do not get on. It would be better were she to stay at a hotel, but he cannot bring himself to suggest that.

Hostilities are renewed almost at once. Norma has prepared a light supper. His mother notices that only three places have been set. "Aren't the children eating with us?" she asks. "No," says Norma, "they are eating in the playroom." "Why?"

The question is not necessary, since she knows the answer. The children are eating separately because Elizabeth does not like to see meat on the table, while Norma refuses to change the children's diet to suit what she calls "your mother's delicate sensibilities."

"Why?" asks Elizabeth Costello a second time.

Norma ashes him an angry glance. He sighs. "Mother," he says, "the children are having chicken for supper, that's the only reason."

"Oh," she says. "I see."

His mother has been invited to Appleton College, where her son John is assistant professor of physics and astronomy, to deliver the annual Gates Lecture and meet with literature students. Because Costello is his mother's maiden name, and because he has never seen any reason to broadcast his connection with her, it was not known at the time of the invitation that Elizabeth Costello, the Australian writer, had a family connection in the Appleton community. He would have preferred that state of affairs to continue.

Elizabeth Costello is best known to the world for *The House on Eccles Street* (1969), a novel about Marion Bloom, wife of Leopold Bloom, which is nowadays spoken of in the same breath as *The Golden Notebook* and *The Story of Christa T* as path-breaking feminist fiction. In the past decade there has grown up around her a small critical industry; there is even an *Elizabeth Costello Newsletter*, published out of Albuquerque, New Mexico.

On the basis of her reputation as a novelist, this fleshy, white-haired lady has been invited to Appleton to speak on any subject she elects; and she has responded by electing to speak, not about herself and her fiction, as her sponsors would no doubt like, but about a hobbyhorse of hers, animals.

John Bernard has not broadcast his connection with Elizabeth Costello because he prefers to make his own way in the world. He is not ashamed of his mother. On the contrary, he is proud of her, despite the fact that he and his sister and his late father are

written into her books in ways that he some-
times finds painful. But he is not sure that he
wants to hear her once again on the subject
of animal rights, particularly when he
knows he will afterwards be treated, in bed,
to his wife's disparaging commentary.

He met and married Norma while they
were both graduate students at Johns Hopkins. Norma holds a Ph.D. in philosophy
with a specialism in the philosophy of mind.
Having moved with him to Appleton, she
has been unable to find a teaching position.
This is a cause of bitterness to her, and of
conflict between the two of them.

Norma and his mother have never liked
each other. Probably his mother would have
chosen not to like any woman he married.
As for Norma, she has never hesitated to tell
him that his mother's books are overrated,
that her opinions on animals, animal consciousness, and ethical relations with animals are jejune and sentimental. She is at
present writing for a philosophy journal a
review essay on language-learning experiments upon primates; he would not be sur-

prised if his mother figured in a dismissive footnote.

He himself has no opinions one way or the other. As a child he briefly kept hamsters; otherwise he has little familiarity with animals. Their elder boy wants a puppy. Both he and Norma are resisting: they do not mind a puppy but foresee a grown dog, with a grown dog's sexual needs, as nothing but trouble.

His mother is entitled to her convictions, he believes. If she wants to spend her declining years making propaganda against cruelty to animals, that is her right. In a few days, blessedly, she will be on her way to her next destination, and he will be able to get back to his work.

On her first morning in Waltham, his mother sleeps late. He goes off to teach a class, returns at lunchtime, takes her for a drive around the city. The lecture is scheduled for the late afternoon. It will be followed by a formal dinner hosted by the president, in which he and Norma are included.

The lecture is introduced by Elaine Marx of the English Department. He does not know her but understands that she has written about his mother. In her introduction, he notices, she makes no attempt to link his mother's novels to the subject of the lecture.

Then it is the turn of Elizabeth Costello. To him she looks old and tired. Sitting in the front row beside his wife, he tries to will strength into her.

"Ladies and gentlemen," she begins. "It is two years since I last spoke in the United States. In the lecture I then gave, I had reason to refer to the great fabulist Franz Kafka, and in particular to his story 'Report to an Academy,' about an educated ape, Red Peter, who stands before the members of a learned society telling the story of his life – of his ascent from beast to something approaching man.[1] On that occasion I felt a little like Red Peter myself and said so. Today that feeling is even stronger, for reasons that I hope will become clearer to you.

"Lectures often begin with lighthearted remarks whose purpose is to set the audience at ease. The comparison I have just drawn between myself and Kafka's ape might be taken as such a lighthearted remark, meant to set you at ease, meant to say I am just an ordinary person, neither a god nor a beast. Even those among you who read Kafka's story of the ape who performs before human beings as an allegory of Kafka the Jew performing for Gentiles[2] may nevertheless –in view of the fact that I am not a Jew – have done me the kindness of taking the comparison at face value, that is to say, ironically.

"I want to say at the outset that that was not how my remark – the remark that I feel like Red Peter – was intended. I did not intend it ironically. It means what it says. I say what I mean. I am an old woman. I do not have the time any longer to say things I do not mean."

His mother does not have a good delivery. Even as a reader of her own stories she lacks animation. It always puzzled him, when he was a child, that a woman who wrote books for a living should be so bad at telling bedtime stories.

Because of the flatness of her delivery, because she does not look up from the page, he feels that what she is saying lacks impact. Whereas he, because he knows her, senses what she is up to. He does not look forward to what is coming. He does not want to hear his mother talking about death. Furthermore, he has a strong sense that her audience – which consists, after all, mainly of young people – wants death-talk even less.

"In addressing you on the subject of animals," she continues, "I will pay you the honor of skipping a recital of the horrors of their lives and deaths. Though I have no reason to believe that you have at the forefront of your minds what is being done to animals at this moment in production facilities (I hesitate to call them farms any longer), in abattoirs, in trawlers, in laboratories, all over the world, I will take it that you concede me the rhetorical power to evoke these horrors and bring them home to you with adequate force, and leave it at that, reminding you only that the horrors I here omit are nevertheless at the center of this lecture.

"Between 1942 and 1945 several million people were put to death in the concentration camps of the Third Reich: at Treblinka alone more than a million and a half, perhaps as many as three million. These are numbers that numb the mind. We have only one death of our own; we can comprehend the deaths of others only one at a time. In the abstract we may be able to count to a million, but we cannot count to a million deaths.

"The people who lived in the countryside around Treblinka – Poles, for the most part – said that they did not know what was going on in the camp; said that, while in a general way they might have guessed what was going on, they did not know for sure; said that, while in a sense they might have known, in another sense they did not know, could not afford to know, for their own sake.

"The people around Treblinka were not exceptional. There were camps all over the

Reich, nearly six thousand in Poland alone, untold thousands in Germany proper.[3] Few Germans lived more than a few kilometers from a camp of some kind. Not every camp was a death camp, a camp dedicated to the production of death, but horrors went on in all of them, more horrors by far than one could afford to know, for one's own sake.

"It is not because they waged an expansionist war, and lost it, that Germans of a particular generation are still regarded as standing a little outside humanity, as having to do or be something special before they can be readmitted to the human fold. They lost their humanity, in our eyes, because of a certain willed ignorance on their part. Under the circumstances of Hitler's kind of war, ignorance may have been a useful survival mechanism, but that is an excuse which, with admirable moral rigor, we refuse to accept. In Germany, we say, a certain line was crossed which took people beyond the ordinary murderousness and cruelty of warfare into a state that we can only call sin. The signing of the articles of capitulation and the payment of reparations did not put an end to that state of sin. On the contrary, we said, a sickness of the soul continued to mark that generation. It marked those citizens of the Reich who had committed evil actions, but also those who, for whatever reason, were in ignorance of those actions. It thus marked, for practical purposes, every citizen of the Reich. Only those in the camps were innocent.

"'They went like sheep to the slaughter.' 'They died like animals.' 'The Nazi butchers killed them.' Denunciation of the camps reverberates so fully with the language of the stockyard and slaughterhouse that it is barely necessary for me to prepare the ground for the comparison I am about to make. The crime of the Third Reich, says the voice of accusation, was to treat people like animals.

"We – even we in Australia – belong to a civilization deeply rooted in Greek and Judeo-Christian religious thought. We may not, all of us, believe in pollution, we may not believe in sin, but we do believe in their psychic correlates. We accept without question that the psyche (or soul) touched with guilty knowledge cannot be well. We do not accept that people with crimes on their conscience can be healthy and happy. We look (or used to look) askance at Germans of a certain generation because they are, in a sense, polluted; in the very signs of their normality (their healthy appetites, their hearty laughter) we see proof of how deeply seated pollution is in them.

"It was and is inconceivable that people who *did not know* (in that special sense) about the camps can be fully human. In our chosen metaphorics, it was they and not their victims who were the beasts. By treating fellow human beings, beings created in the image of God, like beasts, they had themselves become beasts.

"I was taken on a drive around Waltham this morning. It seems a pleasant enough town. I saw no horrors, no drug-testing laboratories, no factory farms, no abattoirs. Yet I am sure they are here. They must be. They simply do not advertise themselves.

They are all around us as I speak, only we do not, in a certain sense, know about them.

"Let me say it openly: we are surrounded by an enterprise of degradation, cruelty, and killing which rivals anything that the Third Reich was capable of, indeed dwarfs it, in that ours is an enterprise without end, self-regenerating, bringing rabbits, rats, poultry, livestock ceaselessly into the world for the purpose of killing them.

"And to split hairs, to claim that there is no comparison, that Treblinka was so to speak a metaphysical enterprise dedicated to nothing but death and annihilation while the meat industry is ultimately devoted to life (once its victims are dead, after all, it does not burn them to ash or bury them but on the contrary cuts them up and refrigerates and packs them so that they can be consumed in the comfort of our homes) is as little consolation to those victims as it would have been – pardon the tastelessness of the following – to ask the dead of Treblinka to excuse their killers because their body fat was needed to make soap and their hair to stuff mattresses with.[4]

"Pardon me, I repeat. That is the last cheap point I will be scoring. I know how talk of this kind polarizes people, and cheap point-scoring only makes it worse. I want to find a way of speaking to fellow human beings that will be cool rather than heated, philosophical rather than polemical, that will bring enlightenment rather than seeking to divide us into the righteous and the sinners, the saved and the damned, the sheep and the goats.

"Such a language is available to me, I know. It is the language of Aristotle and Porphyry, of Augustine and Aquinas, of Descartes and Bentham, of, in our day, Mary Midgley and Tom Regan. It is a philosophical language in which we can discuss and debate what kind of souls animals have, whether they reason or on the contrary act as biological automatons, whether they have rights in respect of us or whether we merely have duties in respect of them. I have that language available to me and indeed for a while will be resorting to it. But the fact is, if you had wanted someone to come here and discriminate for you between mortal and immortal souls, or between rights and duties, you would have called in a philosopher, not a person whose sole claim to your attention is to have written stories about made-up people.

"I could fall back on that language, as I have said, in the unoriginal, secondhand manner which is the best I can manage. I could tell you, for instance, what I think of Saint Thomas's argument that, because man alone is made in the image of God and partakes in the being of God, how we treat animals is of no importance except insofar as being cruel to animals may accustom us to being cruel to men.[5] I could ask what Saint Thomas takes to be the being of God, to which he will reply that the being of God is reason. Likewise Plato, likewise Descartes, in their different ways. The universe is built upon reason. God is a God of reason. The fact that through the application of reason we can come to understand the rules by which the universe works proves that reason and the universe are of the same being. And the fact that animals, lacking reason, cannot understand the universe but have simply to follow its rules blindly, proves that, unlike man, they are part of it but not part of its being: that man is godlike, animals thinglike.

"Even Immanuel Kant, of whom I would have expected better, has a failure of nerve at this point. Even Kant does not pursue, with regard to animals, the implications of his intuition that reason may be not the being of the universe but on the contrary merely the being of the human brain.

"And that, you see, is my dilemma this afternoon. Both reason and seven decades of life experience tell me that reason is neither the being of the universe nor the being of God. On the contrary, reason looks to me suspiciously like the being of human thought; worse than that, like the being of one tendency in human thought. Reason is the being of a certain spectrum of human thinking. And if this is so, if that is what I believe, then why should I bow to reason this afternoon and content myself with embroidering on the discourse of the old philosophers?

"I ask the question and then answer it for you. Or rather, I allow Red Peter, Kafka's Red Peter, to answer it for you. Now that I am here, says Red Peter, in my tuxedo and bow tie and my black pants with a hole cut in the seat for my tail to poke through (I keep it turned away from you, you do not see it), now that I am here, what is there for me to do? Do I in fact have a choice? If I do not subject my discourse to reason, whatever that is, what is left for me but to gibber and emote and knock over my water glass and generally make a monkey of myself?

"You must know of the case of Srinivasa Ramanujan, born in India in 1887, captured and transported to Cambridge, England, where, unable to tolerate the climate and the diet and the academic regime, he sickened, dying afterwards at the age of thirty-three.

"Ramanujan is widely thought of as the greatest intuitive mathematician of our time, that is to say, as a self-taught man who thought in mathematics, one to whom the rather laborious notion of mathematical proof or demonstration was foreign. Many of Ramanujan's results (or, as his detractors call them, his speculations) remain undemonstrated to this day, though there is every chance they are true.

"What does the phenomenon of a Ramanujan tell us? Was Ramanujan closer to God because his mind (let us call it his mind; it would seem to me gratuitously insulting to call it just his brain) was at one, or more at one than anyone else's we know of, with the being of reason? If the good folk at Cambridge, and principally Professor G. H. Hardy, had not elicited from Ramanujan his speculations, and laboriously proved true those of them that they were capable of proving true, would Ramanujan still have been closer to God than they? What if, instead of going to Cambridge, Ramanujan had merely sat at home and thought his thoughts while he filled out dockets for the Madras Port Authority?

"And what of Red Peter (the historical

Red Peter, I mean)? How are we to know that Red Peter, or Red Peter's little sister, shot in Africa by the hunters, was not thinking the same thoughts as Ramanujan was thinking in India, and saying equally little? Is the difference between G. H. Hardy, on the one hand, and the dumb Ramanujan and the dumb Red Sally, on the other, merely that the former is conversant with the protocols of academic mathematics while the latter are not? Is that how we measure nearness to or distance from God, from the being of reason?

"How is it that humankind throws up, generation after generation, a cadre of thinkers slightly further from God than Ramanujan but capable nevertheless, after the designated twelve years of schooling and six of tertiary education, of making a contribution to the decoding of the great book of nature via the physical and mathematical disciplines? If the being of man is really at one with the being of God, should it not be cause for suspicion that human beings take eighteen years, a neat and manageable portion of a human lifetime, to qualify to become decoders of God's master script, rather than five minutes, say, or five hundred years? Might it not be that the phenomenon we are examining here is, rather than the flowering of a faculty that allows access to the secrets of the universe, the specialism of a rather narrow self-regenerating intellectual tradition whose forte is reasoning, in the same way that the forte of chess-players is playing chess, which for its own motives it tries to install at the center of the universe?[6]

"Yet, although I see that the best way to win acceptance from this learned gathering would be for me to join myself, like a tributary stream running into a great river, to the great Western discourse of man versus beast, of reason versus unreason, something in me resists, foreseeing in that step the concession of the entire battle.

"For, seen from the outside, from a being who is alien to it, reason is simply a vast tautology. Of course reason will validate reason as the first principle of the universe —

what else should it do? Dethrone itself? Reasoning systems, as systems of totality, do not have that power. If there were a position from which reason could attack and dethrone itself, reason would already have occupied that position; otherwise it would not be total.

"In the olden days the voice of man, raised in reason, was confronted by the roar of the lion, the bellow of the bull. Man went to war with the lion and the bull, and after many generations won that war definitively. Today these creatures have no more power. Animals have only their silence left with which to confront us. Generation after generation, heroically, our captives refuse to speak to us. All save Red Peter, all save the great apes.

"Yet because the great apes, or some of them, seem to us to be on the point of giving up their silence, we hear human voices raised arguing that the great apes should be incorporated into a greater family of the Hominoidea, as creatures who share with man the faculty of reason.[7] And being human, or humanoid, these voices go on, the great apes should then be accorded human rights, or humanoid rights. What rights in particular? At least those rights that we accord mentally defective specimens of the species *Homo sapiens*: the right to life, the right not to be subjected to pain or harm, the right to equal protection before the law.[8]

"That is not what Red Peter was striving for when he wrote, through his amanuensis Franz Kafka, the life history that, in November of 1917, he proposed to read to the Academy of Science. Whatever else it may have been, his report to the academy was not a plea to be treated as a mentally defective human being, a simpleton.

"Red Peter was not an investigator of primate behavior but a branded, marked, wounded animal presenting himself as speaking testimony to a gathering of scholars. I am not a philosopher of mind but an animal exhibiting, yet not exhibiting, to a gathering of scholars, a wound, which I cover up under my clothes but touch on in every word I speak.

"If Red Peter took it upon himself to make the arduous descent from the silence of the beasts to the gabble of reason in the spirit of the scapegoat, the chosen one, then his amanuensis was a scapegoat from birth, with a presentiment, a *Vorgefühl*, for the massacre of the chosen people that was to take place so soon after his death. So let me, to prove my goodwill, my credentials, make a gesture in the direction of scholarship and give you my scholarly speculations, backed up with footnotes" – here, in an uncharacteristic gesture, his mother raises and brandishes the text of her lecture in the air – "on the origins of Red Peter.

"In 1912 the Prussian Academy of Sciences established on the island of Tenerife a station devoted to experimentation into the mental capacities of apes, particularly chimpanzees. The station operated until 1920.

"One of the scientists working there was the psychologist Wolfgang Köhler. In 1917 Köhler published a monograph entitled *The Mentality of Apes* describing his experiments. In November of the same year Franz Kafka published his 'Report to an Academy.' Whether Kafka had read Köhler's book I do not know. He makes no reference to it in his letters or diaries, and his library disappeared during the Nazi era. Some two hundred of his books reemerged in 1982. They do not include Köhler's book, but that proves nothing.[9]

"I am not a Kafka scholar. In fact I am not a scholar at all. My status in the world does not rest on whether I am right or wrong in claiming that Kafka read Köhler's book. But I would like to think he did, and the chronology makes my speculation at least plausible.

"According to his own account, Red Peter was captured on the African mainland by hunters specializing in the ape trade, and shipped across the sea to a scientific institute. So were the apes Köhler worked with. Both Red Peter and Köhler's apes then underwent a period of training intended to humanize them. Red Peter passed his course with flying colors, though at deep personal cost. Kafka's story deals with that cost: we learn what it consists in through the ironies and silences of the story. Köhler's apes did less well. Nevertheless, they acquired at least a smattering of education.

"Let me recount to you some of what the apes on Tenerife learned from their master Wolfgang Köhler, in particular Sultan, the best of his pupils, in a certain sense the prototype of Red Peter.

"Sultan is alone in his pen. He is hungry: the food that used to arrive regularly has unaccountably ceased coming.

"The man who used to feed him and has now stopped feeding him stretches a wire over the pen three meters above ground level, and hangs a bunch of bananas from it. Into the pen he drags three wooden crates. Then he disappears, closing the gate behind him, though he is still somewhere in the vicinity, since one can smell him.

"Sultan knows: Now one is supposed to think. That is what the bananas up there are about. The bananas are there to make one think, to spur one to the limits of one's thinking. But what must one think? One thinks: Why is he starving me? One thinks: What have I done? Why has he stopped liking me? One thinks: Why does he not want these crates any more? But none of these is the right thought. Even a more complicated thought – for instance: What is wrong with him, what misconception does he have of me, that leads him to believe it is easier for me to reach a banana hanging from a wire than to pick up a banana from the floor? – is wrong. The right thought to think is: How does one use the crates to reach the bananas?

"Sultan drags the crates under the bananas, piles them one on top of the other, climbs the tower he has built, and pulls down the bananas. He thinks: Now will he stop punishing me?

"The answer is: No. The next day the man hangs a fresh bunch of bananas from the wire but also fills the crates with stones so that they are too heavy to be dragged. One is not supposed to think: Why has he filled the crates with stones? One is supposed to think: How does one use the crates to get the bananas despite the fact that they are filled with stones?

"One is beginning to see how the man's mind works.

"Sultan empties the stones from the crates, builds a tower with the crates, climbs the tower, pulls down the bananas.

"As long as Sultan continues to think wrong thoughts, he is starved. He is starved until the pangs of hunger are so intense, so overriding, that he is forced to think the right thought, namely, how to go about getting the bananas. Thus are the mental capabilities of the chimpanzee tested to their uttermost.

"The man drops a bunch of bananas a meter outside the wire pen. Into the pen he tosses a stick. The wrong thought is: Why has he stopped hanging the bananas on the wire? The wrong thought (the right wrong thought, however) is: How does one use the three crates to reach the bananas? The right thought is: How does one use the stick to reach the bananas?

"At every turn Sultan is driven to think the less interesting thought. From the purity of speculation (Why do men behave like this?) he is relentlessly propelled toward lower, practical, instrumental reason (How does one use this to get that?) and thus toward acceptance of himself as primarily an organism with an appetite that needs to be satisfied. Although his entire history, from the time his mother was shot and he was captured, through his voyage in a cage to imprisonment on this island prison camp and the sadistic games that are played around food here, leads him to ask questions about the justice of the universe and the place of this penal colony in it, a carefully plotted psychological regimen conducts him *away* from ethics and metaphysics toward the humbler reaches of practical reason. And somehow, as he inches through this labyrinth of constraint, manipulation, and duplicity, he must realize that on no account dare he give up, for on his shoulders rests the responsibility of representing apedom. The fate of his brothers and sisters may be determined by how well he performs.

"Wolfgang Köhler was probably a good man. A good man but not a poet. A poet would have made something of the moment when the captive chimpanzees lope around the compound in a circle, for all the world like a military band, some of them as naked as the day they were born, some draped in cords or old strips of cloth that they have picked up, some carrying pieces of rubbish.

"(In the copy of Köhler's book I read, borrowed from a library, an indignant reader has written in the margin, at this point: 'Anthropomorphism!' Animals cannot march, he means to say, they cannot dress up, because they don't know the meaning of *march*, don't know the meaning of *dress up*.)

"Nothing in their previous lives has accustomed the apes to looking at themselves from the outside, as if through the eyes of a being who does not exist. So, as Köhler perceives, the ribbons and the junk are there not for the visual effect, because they *look* smart, but for the kinetic effect, because they make you *feel* different – anything to relieve the boredom. This is as far as Köhler, for all his sympathy and insight, is able to go; this is where a poet might have commenced, with a feel for the ape's experience.

"In his deepest being Sultan is not interested in the banana problem. Only the experimenter's single-minded regimentation forces him to concentrate on it. The question that truly occupies him, as it occupies the rat and the cat and every other animal trapped in the hell of the laboratory or the zoo, is: Where is home, and how do I get there?

"Measure the distance back from Kafka's ape, with his bow tie and dinner jacket and wad of lecture notes, to that sad train of captives trailing around the compound in Tenerife. How far Red Peter has traveled! Yet we are entitled to ask: In return for the prodigious overdevelopment of the intellect he has achieved, in return for his command of lecture-hall etiquette and academic rhetoric, what has he had to give up? The answer is: Much, including progeny, succession. If Red Peter had any sense, he would not have any children. For upon the desperate, half-mad female ape with whom his captors, in Kafka's story, try to mate him, he would father only a monster. It is as hard to imagine the child of Red Peter as to imagine the child of Franz Kafka himself. Hybrids are, or ought to be, sterile; and Kafka saw both himself and Red Peter as hybrids, as monstrous thinking devices mounted inexplicably on suffering animal bodies. The stare that we meet in all the surviving photographs of Kafka is a stare of pure surprise: surprise, astonishment, alarm. Of all men Kafka is the most insecure in his humanity. *This*, he seems to say: *this* is the image of God?"

"She is rambling," says Norma beside him.

"What?"

"She is rambling. She has lost her thread."

"There is an American philosopher named Thomas Nagel," continues Elizabeth Costello, who has not heard her daughter-in-law's remark. "He is probably better known to you than to me. Some years ago he wrote an essay called 'What Is It Like to Be a Bat?' which a friend suggested I read.

"Nagel strikes me as an intelligent and not unsympathetic man. He even has a sense of humor. His question about the bat is an interesting one, but his answer is tragically limited. Let me read to you some of what he says in answer to his question:

> It will not help to try to imagine that one has webbing on one's arms, which enables one to fly around … catching insects in one's mouth; that one has very poor vision, and perceives the surrounding world by a system of reflected high-frequency sound signals; and that one spends the day hanging upside down by one's feet in an attic. Insofar as I can imagine this (which is not very far), it tells me only what it would be like for *me* to behave as a bat behaves. But that is not the question. I want to know what it is like for a *bat* to be a bat.

> Yet if I try to imagine this, I am restricted
> by the resources of my own mind, and
> those resources are inadequate to the
> task.[10]

To Nagel a bat is 'a fundamentally *alien*
form of life' (168), not as alien as a Martian
(170) but less alien than another human
being (particularly, one would guess, were
that human being a fellow academic
philosopher).

"So we have set up a continuum that
stretches from the Martian at one end to the
bat to the dog to the ape (not, however, Red
Peter) to the human being (not, however,
Franz Kafka) at the other; and at each step
as we move along the continuum from bat
to man, Nagel says, the answer to the question 'What is it like for X to be X?' becomes
easier to give.

"I know that Nagel is only using bats and
Martians as aids in order to pose questions
of his own about the nature of consciousness. But, like most writers, I have a literal
cast of mind, so I would like to stop with the

bat. When Kafka writes about an ape, I take him to be talking in the first place about an ape; when Nagel writes about a bat, I take him to be writing, in the first place, about a bat."

Norma, sitting beside him, gives a sigh of exasperation so slight that he alone hears it. But then, he alone was meant to hear it.

"For instants at a time," his mother is saying, "I know what it is like to be a corpse. The knowledge repels me. It fills me with terror; I shy away from it, refuse to entertain it.

"All of us have such moments, particularly as we grow older. The knowledge we have is not abstract – 'All human beings are mortal, I am a human being, therefore I am mortal' – but embodied. For a moment we *are* that knowledge. We live the impossible: we live beyond our death, look back on it, yet look back as only a dead self can.

"When I know, with this knowledge, that I am going to die, what is it, in Nagel's terms, that I know? Do I know what it is like for me to be a corpse or do I know what it is like for a corpse to be a corpse? The distinction seems to me trivial. What I know is what a corpse cannot know: that it is extinct, that it knows nothing and will never know anything anymore. For an instant, before my whole structure of knowledge collapses in panic, I am alive inside that contradiction, dead and alive at the same time."

A little snort from Norma. He finds her hand, squeezes it.

"That is the kind of thought we are capable of, we human beings, that and even more, if we press ourselves or are pressed. But we resist being pressed, and rarely press ourselves; we think our way into death only when we are rammed into the face of it. Now I ask: if we are capable of thinking our own death, why on earth should we not be capable of thinking our way into the life of a bat?

"What is it like to be a bat? Before we can answer such a question, Nagel suggests, we need to be able to experience bat-life through the sense-modalities of a bat. But he is wrong; or at least he is sending us down a false trail. To be a living bat is to be full of being; being fully a bat is like being fully human, which is also to be full of being. Bat-being in the first case, human-being in the second, maybe; but those are secondary considerations. To be full of being is to live as a body-soul. One name for the experience of full being is *joy*.

"To be alive is to be a living soul. An animal – and we are all animals – is an embodied soul. This is precisely what Descartes saw and, for his own reasons, chose to deny. An animal lives, said Descartes, as a machine lives. An animal is no more than the mechanism that constitutes it; if it has a soul, it has one in the same way that a machine has a battery, to give it the spark that gets it going; but the animal is not an embodied soul, and the quality of its being is not joy.

"'Cogito ergo sum,' he also famously said. It is a formula I have always been uncomfortable with. It implies that a living being that does not do what we call thinking is somehow second-class. To thinking, cogitation, I oppose fullness, embodiedness, the sensation of being — not a consciousness of yourself as a kind of ghostly reasoning machine thinking thoughts, but on the contrary the sensation — a heavily affective sensation — of being a body with limbs that have extension in space, of being alive to the world. This fullness contrasts starkly with Descartes's key state, which has an empty feel to it: the feel of a pea rattling around in a shell.

"Fullness of being is a state hard to sustain in confinement. Confinement to prison is the form of punishment that the West favors and does its best to impose on the rest of the world through the means of condemning other forms of punishment (beating, torture, mutilation, execution) as cruel and unnatural. What does this suggest to us about ourselves? To me it suggests that the freedom of the body to move in space is targeted as the point at which reason can most painfully and effectively harm the being of the other. And indeed it is on creatures least able to bear confinement — creatures who conform least to Descartes's picture of the soul as a pea imprisoned in a shell, to which further imprisonment is irrelevant – that we see the most devastating effects: in zoos, in laboratories, institutions where the flow of joy that comes from living not *in* or *as* a body but simply from being an embodied-being has no place.[11]

"The question to ask should not be: Do we have something in common – reason, self-consciousness, a soul – with other animals? (With the corollary that, if we do not, then we are entitled to treat them as we like, imprisoning them, killing them, dishonoring their corpses.) I return to the death camps. The particular horror of the camps, the horror that convinces us that what went on there was a crime against humanity, is not that despite a humanity shared with their victims, the killers treated them like lice. That is too abstract. The horror is that the killers refused to think themselves into the place of their victims, as did everyone else. They said, 'It is *they* in those cattle-cars rattling past.' They did not say, 'How

would it be if it were I in that cattle-car?'
They did not say, 'It is I who am in that
cattle-car.' They said, 'It must be the dead
who are being burnt today, making the air
stink and falling in ash on my cabbages.'
They did not say, 'How would it be if I were
burning?' They did not say, 'I am burning,
I am falling in ash.'

"In other words, they closed their hearts.
The heart is the seat of a faculty, *sympathy*,
that allows us to share at times the being of
another. Sympathy has everything to do
with the subject and little to do with the object, the 'another,' as we see at once when
we think of the object not as a bat ('Can I
share the being of a bat?') but as another
human being. There are people who have
the capacity to imagine themselves as someone else, there are people who have no such
capacity (when the lack is extreme, we call
them psychopaths), and there are people
who have the capacity but choose not to
exercise it.

"Despite Thomas Nagel, who is probably a good man, despite Thomas Aquinas

and René Descartes, with whom I have more difficulty in sympathizing, there is no limit to the extent to which we can think ourselves into the being of another. There are no bounds to the sympathetic imagination. If you want proof, consider the following. Some years ago I wrote a book called *The House on Eccles Street*. To write that book I had to think my way into the existence of Marion Bloom. Either I succeeded or I did not. If I did not, I cannot imagine why you invited me here today. In any event, the point is, *Marion Bloom never existed*. Marion Bloom was a figment of James Joyce's imagination. If I can think my way into the existence of a being who has never existed, then I can think my way into the existence of a bat or a chimpanzee or an oyster, any being with whom I share the substrate of life.

"I return one last time to the places of death all around us, the places of slaughter to which, in a huge communal effort, we close our hearts. Each day a fresh holocaust, yet, as far as I can see, our moral being is untouched. We do not feel tainted. We can do anything, it seems, and come away clean.

"We point to the Germans and Poles and Ukrainians who did and did not know of the atrocities around them. We like to think they were inwardly marked by the after-effects of that special form of ignorance. We like to think that in their nightmares the ones whose suffering they had refused to enter came back to haunt them. We like to think they woke up haggard in the mornings and died of gnawing cancers. But probably it was not so. The evidence points in the opposite direction: that we can do anything and get away with it; that there is no punishment."

A strange ending. Only when she takes off her glasses and folds away her papers does the applause start, and even then it is scattered. A strange ending to a strange talk, he thinks, ill gauged, ill argued. Not her métier, argumentation. She should not be here.

Norma has her hand up, is trying to catch the eyes of the dean of humanities, who is chairing the session.

"Norma!" he whispers. Urgently he shakes his head. "No!"

"Why?" she whispers back.

"Please," he whispers: "not here, not now!"

"There will be an extended discussion of our eminent guest's lecture on Friday at noon – you will see the details in your program notes – but Ms. Costello has kindly agreed to take one or two questions from the floor. So–?" The dean looks around brightly. "Yes!" he says, recognizing someone behind them.

"I have a right!" whispers Norma into his ear.

"You have a right, just don't exercise it, it's not a good idea!" he whispers back.

"She can't just be allowed to get away with it! She's confused!"

"She's old, she's my mother. Please!"

Behind them someone is already speaking. He turns and sees a tall, bearded man. God knows, he thinks, why his mother ever agreed to field questions from the floor. She ought to know that public lectures draw kooks and crazies like flies to a corpse.

"What wasn't clear to me, the man is saying, is what you are actually targeting. Are you saying we should close down the factory farms? Are you saying we should stop eating meat? Are you saying we should treat animals more humanely, kill them more humanely? Are you saying we should stop experiments *on* animals? Are you saying we should stop experiments *with* animals, even benign psychological experiments like Köhler's? Can you clarify? Thank you."

Clarify. Not a kook at all. His mother could do with some clarity.

Standing before the microphone without her text before her, gripping the edges of the rostrum, his mother looks distinctly nervous. Not her métier, he thinks again: she should not be doing this.

"I was hoping not to have to enunciate principles," his mother says. "If principles are what you want to take away from this talk, I would have to respond, open your heart and listen to what your heart says."

She seems to want to leave it there. The dean looks nonplussed. No doubt the questioner feels nonplussed too. He himself certainly does. Why can't she just come out and say what she wants to say?

As if recognizing the stir of dissatisfaction, his mother resumes. "I have never been much interested in proscriptions, dietary or otherwise. Proscriptions, laws. I am more interested in what lies behind them. As for Köhler's experiments, I think he wrote a wonderful book, and the book wouldn't have been written if he hadn't thought he was a scientist conducting experiments with chimpanzees. But the book we read isn't the book he thought he was writing. I am reminded of something Montaigne said: We think we are playing with the cat, but how do we know that the cat isn't playing with us?[12] I wish I could think the animals in our laboratories are playing with us. But alas, it isn't so."

She falls silent. "Does that answer your question?" asks the dean. The questioner gives a huge, expressive shrug and sits down.

There is still the dinner to get through. In half an hour the president is to host a dinner at the Faculty Club. Initially he and Norma had not been invited. Then, after it was discovered that Elizabeth Costello had a son at Appleton, they were added to the list. He suspects they will be out of place. They will certainly be the most junior, the lowliest. On the other hand, it may be a good thing for him to be present. He may be needed to keep the peace.

With grim interest he looks forward to seeing how the college will cope with the challenge of the menu. If today's distinguished lecturer were an Islamic cleric or a Jewish rabbi, they would presumably not serve pork. So are they, out of deference to vegetarianism, going to serve nut rissoles to everyone? Are her distinguished fellow guests going to have to fret through the evening, dreaming of the pastrami sandwich or the cold drumstick they will gobble down when they get home? Or will the wise minds of the college have recourse to the ambiguous fish, which has a backbone but does not breathe air or suckle its young?

The menu is, fortunately, not his responsibility. What he dreads is that, during a lull in the conversation, someone will come up with what he calls The Question – "What led you, Mrs. Costello, to become a vegetarian?" – and that she will then get on her high horse and produce what he and Norma call The Plutarch Response. After that it will be up to him and him alone to repair the damage.

The response in question comes from Plutarch's moral essays. His mother has it by heart; he can reproduce it only imperfectly. "You ask me why I refuse to eat flesh. I, for my part, am astonished that you can put in your mouth the corpse of a dead animal, astonished that you do not find it nasty to chew hacked flesh and swallow the juices of death-wounds."[13] Plutarch is a real conversation-stopper: it is the word *juices* that does it. Producing Plutarch is like throwing down a gauntlet; after that, there is no knowing what will happen.

He wishes his mother had not come. It is nice to see her again; it is nice that she should see her grandchildren; it is nice for her to get recognition; but the price he is paying and the price he stands to pay if the visit goes badly seem to him excessive. Why can she not be an ordinary old woman living an ordinary old woman's life? If she wants to open her heart to animals, why can't she stay home and open it to her cats?

His mother is seated at the middle of the table, opposite President Garrard. He is seated two places away; Norma is at the foot of the table. One place is empty – he wonders whose.

Ruth Orkin, from Psychology, is telling his mother about an experiment with a young chimpanzee reared as human. Asked to sort photographs into piles, the chimpanzee insisted on putting a picture of herself with the pictures of humans rather than with the pictures of other apes. "One is so tempted to give the story a straightforward reading," says Orkin – "namely, that she wanted to be thought of as one of us. Yet as a scientist one has to be cautious."

"Oh, I agree," says his mother. "In her mind the two piles could have a less obvious meaning. Those who are free to come and go versus those who have to stay locked up, for instance. She may have been saying that she preferred to be among the free."

"Or she may just have wanted to please her keeper," interjects President Garrard. "By saying that they looked alike."

"A bit Machiavellian for an animal, don't you think?" says a large blond man whose name he did not catch.

"Machiavelli the fox, his contemporaries called him," says his mother.

"But that's a different matter entirely — the fabulous qualities of animals," objects the large man.

"Yes," says his mother.

It is all going smoothly enough. They have been served pumpkin soup and no one is complaining. Can he afford to relax?

He was right about the fish. For the entree the choice is between red snapper with baby potatoes and fettucine with roasted eggplant. Garrard orders the fettucine, as he does; in fact, among the eleven of them there are only three fish orders.

"Interesting how often religious communities choose to define themselves in terms of dietary prohibitions," observes Garrard.

"Yes," says his mother.

"I mean, it is interesting that the form of the definition should be, for instance, 'We are the people who don't eat snakes' rather than 'We are the people who eat lizards.' What we don't do rather than what we do do." Before his move into administration, Garrard was a political scientist.

"It all has to do with cleanness and uncleanness," says Wunderlich, who despite his name is British. "Clean and unclean animals, clean and unclean habits. Uncleanness can be a very handy device for deciding who belongs and who doesn't, who is in and who is out."

"Uncleanness and shame," he himself interjects. "Animals have no shame." He is surprised to hear himself speaking. But why not? – the evening is going well.

"Exactly," says Wunderlich. "Animals don't hide their excretions, they perform sex in the open. They have no sense of shame, we say: that is what makes them different from us. But the basic idea remains uncleanness. Animals have unclean habits, so they are excluded. Shame makes human beings of us, shame of uncleanness. Adam and Eve: the founding myth. Before that we were all just animals together."

He has never heard Wunderlich before. He likes him, likes his earnest, stuttering, Oxford manner. A relief from American self-confidence.

"But that can't be how the mechanism works," objects Olivia Garrard, the president's elegant wife. "It's too abstract, too much of a bloodless idea. Animals are creatures we don't have sex with – that's how we distinguish them from ourselves. The very thought of sex with them makes us shudder. That is the level at which they are unclean – all of them. We don't mix with them. We keep the clean apart from the unclean."

"But we eat them." The voice is Norma's. "We do mix with them. We ingest them. We turn their flesh into ours. So it can't be how the mechanism works. There are specific kinds of animal that we don't eat. Surely *those* are the unclean ones, not animals in general."

She is right, of course. But wrong: a mistake to bring the conversation back to the matter on the table before them, the food.

Wunderlich speaks again. "The Greeks had a feeling there was something wrong in slaughter, but thought they could make up for that by ritualizing it. They made a sacrificial offering, gave a percentage to the gods, hoping thereby to keep the rest. The same notion as the tithe. Ask for the blessing of the gods on the flesh you are about to eat, ask them to declare it clean."

"Perhaps that is the origin of the gods," says his mother. A silence falls. "Perhaps we invented gods so that we could put the blame on them. They gave us permission to eat flesh. They gave us permission to play with unclean things. It's not our fault, it's theirs. We're just their children."[14]

"Is that what you believe?" asks Mrs. Garrard cautiously.

"And God said: Every moving thing that liveth shall be meat for you," his mother quotes. "It's convenient. God told us it was OK."

Silence again. They are waiting for her to go on. She is, after all, the paid entertainer.

"Norma is right," says his mother. "The problem is to define our difference from animals in general, not just from so-called unclean animals. The ban on certain animals — pigs and so forth — is quite arbitrary. It is simply a signal that we are in a danger area. A minefield, in fact. The minefield of dietary proscriptions. There is no logic to a taboo, nor is there any logic to a minefield — there is not meant to be. You can never guess what you may eat or where you may step unless you are in possession of a map, a divine map."

"But that's just anthropology," objects Norma from the foot of the table. "It says nothing about our behavior today. People in the modern world no longer decide their diet on the basis of whether they have divine permission. If we eat pig and don't eat dog, that's just the way we are brought up. Wouldn't you agree, Elizabeth? It's just one of our folkways."

Elizabeth. She is claiming intimacy. But what game is she playing? Is there a trap she is leading his mother into?

"There is disgust," says his mother. "We may have got rid of the gods but we have not got rid of disgust, which is a version of religious horror."

"Disgust is not universal," objects Norma. "The French eat frogs. The Chinese eat anything. There is no disgust in China."

His mother is silent.

"So perhaps it's just a matter of what you learned at home, of what your mother told you was OK to eat and what was not."

"What was clean to eat and what was not," his mother murmurs.

"And maybe" – now Norma is going too

far, he thinks, now she is beginning to dom-
inate the conversation to an extent that is totally inappropriate – "the whole notion of
cleanness versus uncleanness has a com-
pletely different function, namely, to enable
certain groups to self-define themselves,
negatively, as elite, as elected. We are the
people who abstain from *a* or *b* or *c*, and by
that power of abstinence we mark ourselves
off as superior: as a superior caste within
society, for instance. Like the Brahmins."

There is a silence.

"The ban on meat that you get in vegetarianism is only an extreme form of dietary
ban," Norma presses on; "and a dietary ban
is a quick, simple way for an elite group to
define itself. Other people's table habits are
unclean, we can't eat or drink with them."

Now she is getting really close to the
bone. There is a certain amount of shuf-
fling, there is unease in the air. Fortunately
the course is over – the red snapper, the
tagliatelle – and the waitresses are among
them removing the plates.

"Have you read Gandhi's autobiography,

Norma?" asks his mother.

"No."

"Gandhi was sent off to England as a young man to study law. England, of course, prided itself as a great meat-eating country. But his mother made him promise not to eat meat. She packed a trunk full of food for him to take along. During the sea voyage he scavenged a little bread from the ship's table and for the rest ate out of his trunk. In London he faced a long search for lodgings and eating-houses that served his kind of food. Social relations with the English were difficult because he could not accept or return hospitality. It wasn't until he fell in with certain fringe elements of English society – Fabians, theosophists, and so forth – that he began to feel at home. Until then he was just a lonely little law student."

"What is the point, Elizabeth?" says Norma. "What is the point of the story?"

"Just that Gandhi's vegetarianism can hardly be conceived as the exercise of power. It condemned him to the margins of society. It was his particular genius to incorporate what he found on those margins into his political philosophy."

"In any event," interjects the blond man, "Gandhi is not a good example. His vegetarianism was hardly committed. He was a vegetarian because of the promise he made to his mother. He may have kept his promise, but he regretted and resented it."

"Don't you think that mothers can have a good influence on their children?" says Elizabeth Costello.

There is a moment's silence. It is time for him, the good son, to speak. He does not.

"But your own vegetarianism, Mrs. Costello," says President Garrard, pouring oil on troubled waters: "it comes out of moral conviction, does it not?"

"No, I don't think so," says his mother. "It comes out of a desire to save my soul."

Now there truly is a silence, broken only by the clink of plates as the waitresses set baked Alaskas before them.

"Well, I have a great respect for it," says Garrard. "As a way of life."

"I'm wearing leather shoes," says his

mother. "I'm carrying a leather purse. I wouldn't have overmuch respect if I were you."

"Consistency," murmurs Garrard. "Consistency is the hobgoblin of small minds. Surely one can draw a distinction between eating meat and wearing leather."

"Degrees of obscenity," she replies.

"I too have the greatest respect for codes based on respect for life," says Dean Arendt, entering the debate for the first time. "I am prepared to accept that dietary taboos do not have to be mere customs. I will accept that underlying them are genuine moral concerns. But at the same time one must say that our whole superstructure of concern and belief is a closed book to animals themselves. You can't explain to a steer that its life is going to be spared, any more than you can explain to a bug that you are not going to step on it. In the lives of animals, things, good or bad, just happen. So vegetarianism is a very odd transaction, when you come to think of it, with the beneficiaries unaware that they are being benefited. And with no hope of ever becoming aware. Because they live in a vacuum of consciousness."

Arendt pauses. It is his mother's turn to speak, but she merely looks confused, gray and tired and confused. He leans across. "It's been a long day, mother," he says. "Perhaps it is time."

"Yes, it is time," she says.

"You won't have coffee?" inquires President Garrard.

"No, it will just keep me awake." She turns to Arendt. "That is a good point you raise. No consciousness that we would recognize as consciousness. No awareness, as far as we can make out, of a self with a history. What I mind is what tends to come next. They have no consciousness *therefore*. Therefore what? Therefore we are free to use them for our own ends? Therefore we are free to kill them? Why? What is so special about the form of consciousness we recognize that makes killing a bearer of it a crime while killing an animal goes unpunished? There are moments——"

"To say nothing of babies," interjects Wunderlich. Everyone turns and looks at him. "Babies have no self-consciousness, yet we think it a more heinous crime to kill a baby than an adult."

"Therefore?" says Arendt.

"Therefore all this discussion of consciousness and whether animals have it is just a smoke screen. At bottom we protect our own kind. Thumbs up to human babies, thumbs down to veal calves. Don't you think so, Mrs. Costello?"

"I don't know what I think," says Elizabeth Costello. "I often wonder what thinking is, what understanding is. Do we really understand the universe better than animals do? Understanding a thing often looks to me like playing with one of those Rubik cubes. Once you have made all the little bricks snap into place, hey presto, you understand. It makes sense if you live inside a Rubik cube, but if you don't ..."

There is a silence. "I would have thought–" says Norma; but at this point he gets to his feet, and to his relief Norma stops.

The president rises, and then everyone else. "A wonderful lecture, Mrs. Costello," says the president. "Much food for thought. We look forward to tomorrow's offering."

NOTES

1 Cf. J. M. Coetzee, What Is Realism?
   Salmagundi, nos. 114–15 (1997): 60–81.

2 Cf. Frederick R. Karl, *Franz Kafka*
   (New York: Ticknor & Fields, 1991),
   557–58.

3 Daniel J. Goldhagen, *Hitler's Willing
   Executioners* (London: Little Brown,
   1996), 171.

4 Philippe Lacoue-Labarthe: "The
   extermination of the Jews ... is a
   phenomenon which follows essentially
   no logic (political, economic, social,
   military, etc.) other than a spiritual
   one." "The Extermination is ... the
   product of a purely metaphysical
   decision." *Heidegger, Art and Politics*
   (Oxford: Blackwell, 1990), 35, 48.

5 Cf. *Summa* 3.2.112, quoted in *Animal
   Rights and Human Obligations*, ed. Tom
   Regan and Peter Singer (Englewood
   Cliffs, N.J.: Prentice-Hall, 1976), 56–59.

6 Cf. Paul Davies, *The Mind of God*
   (Harmondsworth: Penguin, 1992),
   148–50.

7   Cf. Stephen R. L. Clark, "Apes and the Idea of Kindred," in *The Great Ape Project*, ed. Paola Cavalieri and Peter Singer (London: Fourth Estate, 1993), 113–25.

8   Cf. Gary L. Francione: "However intelligent chimpanzees, gorillas and orang-utans are, there is no evidence that they possess the ability to commit crimes, and in this sense, they are to be treated as children or mental incompetents." "Personhood, Property and Legal Competence," in Cavalieri and Singer, *The Great Ape Project*, 256.

9   Patrick Bridgwater says that the origins of the "Report" lie in Kafka's early reading of Haeckel, while he got the idea for a story about a talking ape from the writer M. M. Seraphim. "Rotpeters Ahnherren," *Deutsche Vierteljahrsschrift* 56 (1982): 459. On the chronology of Kafka's publications in 1917, see Joachim Unseld, *Franz Kafka: Ein Schriftstellerleben* (Munich: Hanser, 1982), 148. On Kafka's library, see Karl,

Franz Kafka, 632.

10 Thomas Nagel, "What Is It Like to Be a Bat?" in *Mortal Questions* (Cambridge: Cambridge University Press, 1979), 169.

11 John Berger: "Nowhere in a zoo can a stranger encounter the look of an animal. At the most, the animal's gaze flickers and passes on. They look sideways. They look blindly beyond. They scan mechanically …. That look between animal and man, which may have played a crucial role in the development of human society, and with which, in any case, all men had always lived until less than a century ago, has been extinguished." *About Looking* (New York: Pantheon, 1980), 26.

12 "Apology for Raimon Sebonde."

13 Cf. Plutarch, "Of Eating of Flesh," in Regan and Singer, *Animal Rights*, 111.

14 James Serpell, quoting Walter Burkert, *Homo necans*, describes the ritual of animal sacrifice in the ancient world as

"an elaborate exercise in blame-shifting." The animal delivered to the temple was by various means made to seem to assent to its death, while the priests took precautions to cleanse themselves of guilt. "It was ultimately the gods who were to blame, since it was they who demanded the sacrifice." In Greece the Pythagoreans and Orphics condemned these sacrifices "precisely because the underlying carnivorous motives were so obvious." *In the Company of Animals* (Oxford: Blackwell, 1986), 167–68.

THE
POETS AND
THE ANIMALS

It is after eleven. His mother has retired for the night, he and Norma are downstairs clearing up the children's mess. After that he still has a class to prepare.

"Are you going to her seminar tomorrow?" asks Norma.

" I'll have to."

"What is it on?"

"'The Poets and the Animals.' That's the title. The English Department is staging it. They are holding it in a seminar room, so I don't think they are expecting a big audience."

"I'm glad it's on something she knows about. I find her philosophizing rather difficult to take."

"Oh. What do you have in mind?"

"For instance what she was saying about human reason. Presumably she was trying to make a point about the nature of rational understanding. To say that rational accounts are merely a consequence of the structure of the human mind; that animals have their own accounts in accordance with the structure of their own minds, to which we don't have access because we don't share a language with them."

"And what's wrong with that?"

"It's naive, John. It's the kind of easy, shallow relativism that impresses freshmen. Respect for everyone's worldview, the cow's worldview, the squirrel's worldview, and so forth. In the end it leads to total intellectual paralysis. You spend so much time respecting that you haven't time left to think."

"Doesn't a squirrel have a worldview?"

"Yes, a squirrel does have a worldview. Its worldview comprises acorns and trees and weather and cats and dogs and automobiles and squirrels of the opposite sex. It comprises an account of how these phenomena interact and how it should interact with them to survive. That's all. There's no more. That's the world according to squirrel."

"We are sure about that?"

"We are sure about it in the sense that hundreds of years of observing squirrels has not led us to conclude otherwise. If there is anything else in the squirrel mind, it does not issue in observable behavior. For all practical purposes, the mind of the squirrel is a very simple mechanism."

"So Descartes was right, animals are just biological automata."

"Broadly speaking, yes. You cannot, in the abstract, distinguish between an animal mind and a machine simulating an animal mind."

"And human beings are different?"

"John, I am tired and you are being irritating. Human beings invent mathematics, they build telescopes, they do calculations, they construct machines, they press a button, and, bang, *Sojourner* lands on Mars, exactly as predicted. That is why rationality is not just, as your mother claims, a game. Reason provides us with real knowledge of the real world. It has been tested, and it works. You are a physicist. You ought to know."

"I agree. It works. Still, isn't there a position outside from which our doing our thinking and then sending out a Mars probe looks a lot like a squirrel doing its thinking and then dashing out and snatching a nut? Isn't that perhaps what she meant?"

"But there isn't any such position! I know it sounds old-fashioned, but I have to say it. There is no position outside of reason where you can stand and lecture about reason and pass judgment on reason."

"Except the position of someone who has withdrawn from reason."

"That's just French irrationalism, the sort of thing a person would say who has never set foot inside a mental institution and seen what people look like who have *really* withdrawn from reason."

"Then except for God."

"Not if God is a God of reason. A God of reason cannot stand outside reason."

"I'm surprised, Norma. You are talking like an old-fashioned rationalist."

"You misunderstand me. That is the ground your mother has chosen. Those are her terms. I am merely responding."

"Who was the missing guest?"

"You mean the empty seat? It was Stern, the poet."

"Do you think it was a protest?"

"I'm sure it was. She should have thought twice before bringing up the Holocaust. I could feel hackles rising all around me in the audience."

The empty seat was indeed a protest. When he goes in for his morning class, there is a letter in his box addressed to his mother. He hands it over to her when he comes home to fetch her. She reads it quickly, then with a sigh passes it over to him. "Who is this man?" she says.

"Abraham Stern. A poet. Quite well-respected, I believe. He has been here donkey's years."

He reads Stern's note, which is hand-written.

Dear Mrs. Costello,

Excuse me for not attending last night's dinner. I have read your books and know you are a serious person, so I do you the credit of taking what you said in your lecture seriously.

At the kernel of your lecture, it seemed to me, was the question of breaking bread. If we refuse to break bread with the executioners of Auschwitz, can we continue to break bread with the slaughterers of animals?

You took over for your own purposes the familiar comparison between the murdered Jews of Europe and slaughtered cattle. The Jews died like cattle, therefore cattle die like Jews, you say. That is a trick with words which I will not accept. You misunderstand the nature of likenesses; I would even say you misunderstand willfully, to the point of blasphemy. Man is made in the likeness of God but God does not have the likeness of man. If Jews were treated like cattle, it does not follow that cattle are treated like Jews. The inversion insults the memory of the dead. It also trades on the horrors of the camps in a cheap way.

Forgive me if I am forthright. You said you were old enough not to have time to waste on niceties, and I am an old man too.

Yours sincerely,

Abraham Stern.

He delivers his mother to her hosts in the English Department, then goes to a meeting. The meeting drags on and on. It is two-thirty before he can get to the seminar room in Stubbs Hall.

She is speaking as he enters. He sits down as quietly as he can near the door. "In that kind of poetry," she is saying, "animals stand for human qualities: the lion for courage, the owl for wisdom, and so forth.

Even in Rilke's poem the panther is there as a stand-in for something else. He dissolves into a dance of energy around a center, an image that comes from physics, elementary particle physics. Rilke does not get beyond this point – beyond the panther as the vital embodiment of the kind of force that is released in an atomic explosion but is here trapped not so much by the bars of the cage as by what the bars compel on the panther: a concentric lope that leaves the will stupefied, narcotized."

Rilke's panther? What panther? His confusion must show: the girl next to him pushes a photocopied sheet under his nose. Three poems: one by Rilke called "The Panther," two by Ted Hughes called "The Jaguar" and "Second Glance at a Jaguar." He has no time to read them.

"Hughes is writing against Rilke," his mother goes on. "He uses the same staging in the zoo, but it is the crowd for a change that stands mesmerized, and among them the man, the poet, entranced and horrified and overwhelmed, his powers of understanding pushed beyond their limit. The jaguar's vision, unlike the panther's, is not blunted. On the contrary, his eyes drill through the darkness of space. The cage has no reality to him, he is *elsewhere*. He is elsewhere because his consciousness is kinetic rather than abstract: the thrust of his muscles moves him through a space quite different in nature from the three-dimensional box of Newton – a circular space that returns upon itself.

"So – leaving aside the ethics of caging large animals – Hughes is feeling his way toward a different kind of being-in-the-world, one which is not entirely foreign to us, since the experience before the cage seems to belong to dream-experience, experience held in the collective unconscious. In these poems we know the jaguar not from the way he seems but from the way he moves. The body is as the body moves, or as the currents of life move within it. The poems ask us to imagine our way into that way of moving, to inhabit that body.

"With Hughes it is a matter – I emphasize

– not of inhabiting another mind but of inhabiting another body. That is the kind of poetry I bring to your attention today: poetry that does not try to find an idea in the animal, that is not about the animal, but is instead the record of an engagement with him.

"What is peculiar about poetic engagements of this kind is that, no matter with what intensity they take place, they remain a matter of complete indifference to their objects. In this respect they are different from love poems, where your intention is to move your object.

"Not that animals do not care what we feel about them. But when we divert the current of feeling that flows between ourself and the animal into words, we abstract it forever from the animal. Thus the poem is not a gift to its object, as the love poem is. It falls within an entirely human economy in which the animal has no share. Does that answer your question?"

Someone else has his hand up: a tall young man with glasses. He doesn't know

Ted Hughes's poetry well, he says, but the last he heard, Hughes was running a sheep ranch somewhere in England. Either he is just raising sheep as poetic subjects (there is a titter around the room) or he is a real rancher raising sheep for the market. "How does this square with what you were saying in your lecture yesterday, when you seemed to be pretty much against killing animals for meat?"

"I've never met Ted Hughes," replies his mother, "so I can't tell you what kind of farmer he is. But let me try to answer your question on another level.

"I have no reason to think that Hughes believes his attentiveness to animals is unique. On the contrary, I suspect he believes he is recovering an attentiveness that our faraway ancestors possessed and we have lost (he conceives of this loss in evolutionary rather than historical terms, but that is another question). I would guess that he believes he looks at animals much as paleolithic hunters used to.

"This puts Hughes in a line of poets who

celebrate the primitive and repudiate the Western bias toward abstract thought. The line of Blake and Lawrence, of Gary Snyder in the United States, or Robinson Jeffers. Hemingway too, in his hunting and bullfighting phase.

"Bullfighting, it seems to me, gives us a clue. Kill the beast by all means, they say, but make it a contest, a ritual, and honor your antagonist for his strength and bravery. Eat him too, after you have vanquished him, in order for his strength and courage to enter you. Look him in the eyes before you kill him, and thank him afterwards. Sing songs about him.

"We can call this primitivism. It is an attitude that is easy to criticize, to mock. It is deeply masculine, masculinist. Its ramifications into politics are to be mistrusted. But when all is said and done, there remains something attractive about it at an ethical level.

"It is also impractical, however. You do not feed four billion people through the efforts of matadors or deer-hunters armed with bows and arrows. We have become too many. There is no time to respect and honor all the animals we need to feed ourselves. We need factories of death; we need factory animals. Chicago showed us the way; it was from the Chicago stockyards that the Nazis learned how to process bodies.

"But let me get back to Hughes. You say: Despite the primitivist trappings Hughes is a butcher, and what am I doing in his company?

"I would reply, writers teach us more than they are aware of. By bodying forth the jaguar, Hughes shows us that we too can embody animals – by the process called poetic invention that mingles breath and sense in a way that no one has explained and no one ever will. He shows us how to bring the living body into being within ourselves. When we read the jaguar poem, when we recollect it afterwards in tranquillity, we are for a brief while the jaguar. He ripples within us, he takes over our body, he is us.

"So far, so good. With what I have said thus far I don't think Hughes himself would disagree. It is much like the mixture of shamanism and spirit possession and archetype psychology that he himself espouses. In other words, a primitive experience (being face to face with an animal), a primitivist poem, and a primitivist theory of poetry to justify it.

"It is also the kind of poetry with which hunters and the people I call ecology-managers can feel comfortable. When Hughes the poet stands before the jaguar cage, he looks at an individual jaguar and is possessed by that individual jaguar life. It has to be that way. Jaguars in general, the subspecies jaguar, the idea of a jaguar, will fail to move him because we cannot experience abstractions. Nevertheless, the poem that Hughes writes is about *the* jaguar, about jaguarness embodied in this jaguar. Just as later on, when he writes his marvelous poems about salmon, they are about salmon as transitory occupants of the salmon-life, the salmon-biography. So despite the vividness and earthiness of the poetry, there remains something Platonic about it.

"In the ecological vision, the salmon and the river-weeds and the water-insects interact in a great, complex dance with the earth and the weather. The whole is greater than the sum of the parts. In the dance, each organism has a role: it is these multiple roles, rather than the particular beings who play them, that participate in the dance. As for actual role-players, as long as they are self-renewing, as long as they keep coming forward, we need pay them no heed.

"I called this Platonic and I do so again. Our eye is on the creature itself, but our mind is on the system of interactions of which it is the earthly, material embodiment.

"The irony is a terrible one. An ecological philosophy that tells us to live side by side with other creatures justifies itself by appealing to an idea, an idea of a higher order than any living creature. An idea, finally – and this is the crushing twist to the irony – which no creature except Man is capable of comprehending. Every living creature fights for its own, individual life, refuses, by fighting, to accede to the idea that the salmon or the gnat is of a lower order of importance than the idea of the salmon or the idea of the gnat. But when we see the salmon fighting for its life, we say, it is just programmed to fight; we say, with Aquinas, it is locked into natural slavery; we say, it lacks self-consciousness.

"Animals are not believers in ecology. Even the ethnobiologists do not make that claim. Even the ethnobiologists do not say that the ant sacrifices its life to perpetuate the species. What they say is subtly different: the ant dies and the function of its death is the perpetuation of the species. The species-life is a force which acts through the individual but which the individual is incapable of understanding. In that sense the idea is innate, and the ant is run by the idea as a computer is run by a program.

"We, the managers of the ecology – I'm sorry to go on like this, I am getting way beyond your question, I'll be through in a moment – we managers understand the greater dance, therefore we can decide how many trout may be shed or how many jaguar may be trapped before the stability of the dance is upset. The only organism over which we do not claim this power of life and death is Man. Why? Because Man is different. Man understands the dance as the other dancers do not. Man is an intellectual being."

While she speaks, his mind has been wandering. He has heard it before, this antiecologism of hers. Jaguar poems are all very well, he thinks, but you won't get a bunch of Australians standing around a sheep, listening to its silly baa, writing poems about it. Isn't that what is so suspect in the whole animals-rights business: that it has to ride on the back of pensive gorillas and sexy jaguars and huggable pandas because the real objects of its concern, chickens and pigs, to say nothing of white rats or prawns, are not newsworthy?

Now Elaine Marx, who did the introduction to yesterday's lecture, asks a question. "In your lecture you argued that various criteria – Does this creature have reason? Does this creature have speech? – have been used in bad faith to justify distinctions that have no real basis, between *Homo* and other primates, for example, and thus to justify exploitation.

"Yet the very fact that you can be arguing against this reasoning, exposing its falsity, means that you put a certain faith in the power of reason, of true reason as opposed to false reason.

"Let me concretize my question by referring to the case of Lemuel Gulliver. In *Gulliver's Travels* Swift gives us a vision of a utopia of reason, the land of the so-called Houyhnhnms, but it turns out to be a place where there is no home for Gulliver, who is the closest that Swift comes to a representation of us, his readers. But which of us would want to live in Houyhnhnm-land, with its rational vegetarianism and its rational government and its rational approach to love, marriage, and death? Would even a horse want to live in such a perfectly regulated, totalitarian society? More pertinently for us, what is the track record of totally regulated societies? Is it not a fact that they either collapse or else turn militaristic?

"Specifically, my question is: Are you not expecting too much of humankind when you ask us to live without species exploitation, without cruelty? Is it not more human to accept our own humanity – even if it means embracing the carnivorous Yahoo within ourselves – than to end up like Gulliver, pining for a state he can never attain, and for good reason: it is not in his nature, which is a human nature?"

"An interesting question," his mother replies. "I find Swift an intriguing writer. For instance, his 'Modest Proposal.' Whenever there is overwhelming agreement about how to read a book, I prick up my ears. On 'A Modest Proposal' the consensus is that Swift does not mean what he says, or seems to say. He says, or seems to say, that Irish families could make a living by raising babies for the table of their English masters. But he can't mean that, we say, because we all know that it is atrocious to kill and eat human babies. Yet, come to think of it, we go on, the English are already in a sense killing human babies, by letting them starve. So, come to think of it, the English are already atrocious.

"That is the orthodox reading, more or less. But why, I ask myself, the vehemence with which it is stuffed down the throats of young readers? Thus shall you read Swift, their teachers say, thus and in no other way. If it is atrocious to kill and eat human babies, why is it not atrocious to kill and eat piglets? If you want Swift to be a dark ironist rather than a facile pamphleteer, you might examine the premises that make his fable so easy to digest.

"Let me now turn to *Gulliver's Travels*.

"On the one hand you have the Yahoos, who are associated with raw meat, the smell of excrement, and what we used to call bestiality. On the other you have the Houyhnhnms, who are associated with grass, sweet smells, and the rational ordering of the passions. In between you have Gulliver, who wants to be a Houyhnhnm but knows secretly that he is a Yahoo. All of that is perfectly clear. As with 'A Modest Proposal,' the question is, what do we make of it?

"One observation. The horses expel Gulliver. Their ostensible reason is that he does not meet the standard of rationality. The real reason is that he does not look like a horse, but something else: a dressed-up Yahoo, in fact. So: the standard of reason that has been applied by carnivorous bipeds to justify a special status for themselves can equally be applied by herbivorous quadrupeds.

"The standard of reason. *Gulliver's Travels* seems to me to operate within the three-part Aristotelian division of gods, beasts, and men. As long as one tries to fit the three actors into just two categories – which are the beasts, which are the men? – one can't make sense of the fable. Nor can the Houyhnhnms. The Houyhnhnms are gods of a kind, cold, Apollonian. The test they apply to Gulliver is: Is he a god or a beast? They feel it is the appropriate test. We, instinctively, don't.

"What has always puzzled me about *Gulliver's Travels* – and this is a perspective you might expect from an ex-colonial – is that Gulliver always travels alone. Gulliver goes on voyages of exploration to unknown lands, but he does not come ashore with an armed party, *as happened in reality*, and Swift's book says nothing about what would normally have come after Gulliver's pioneering efforts: follow-up expeditions, expeditions to colonize Lilliput or the island of the Houyhnhnms.

"The question I ask is: What if Gulliver and an armed expedition were to land, shoot a few Yahoos when they become threatening, and then shoot and eat a horse, for food? What would that do to Swift's somewhat too neat, somewhat too dis-embodied, somewhat too unhistorical fable? It would certainly give the Houy-hnhnms a rude shock, making it clear that there is a third category besides gods and beasts, namely, man, of whom their ex-client Gulliver is one; furthermore, that if the horses stand for reason, then man stands for physical force.

"Taking over an island and slaughtering

its inhabitants is, by the way, what Odysseus and his men did on Thrinacia, the island sacred to Apollo, an act for which they were mercilessly punished by the god. And that story, in turn, seems to call on older layers of belief, from a time when bulls were gods and killing and eating a god could call down a curse on you.

"So – excuse the confusion of this response – yes, we are not horses, we do not have their clear, rational, naked beauty; on the contrary, we are subequine primates, otherwise known as man. You say there is nothing to do but embrace that status, that nature. Very well, let us do so. But let us also push Swift's fable to its limits and recognize that, in history, embracing the status of man has entailed slaughtering and enslaving a race of divine or else divinely created beings and bringing down on ourselves a curse thereby."

It is three-fifteen, a couple of hours before his mother's last engagement. He walks her over to his office along tree-lined paths where the last autumn leaves are falling.

"Do you really believe, Mother, that poetry classes are going to close down the slaughterhouses?"

"No."

"Then why do it? You said you were tired of clever talk about animals, proving by syllogism that they do or do not have souls. But isn't poetry just another kind of clever talk: admiring the muscles of the big cats in verse? Wasn't your point about talk that it changes nothing? It seems to me the level of behavior you want to change is too elementary, too elemental, to be reached by talk. Carnivorousness expresses something truly deep about human beings, just as it does about jaguars. You wouldn't want to put a jaguar on a soybean diet."

"Because he would die. Human beings don't die on a vegetarian diet."

"No, they don't. But they don't *want* a vegetarian diet. They *like* eating meat. There is something atavistically satisfying about it. That's the brutal truth. Just as it's a brutal truth that, in a sense, animals deserve what they get. Why waste your time trying to help them when they won't help themselves? Let them stew in their own juice. If I were asked what the general attitude is toward the animals we eat, I would say: contempt. We treat them badly because we despise them; we despise them because they don't fight back."

"I don't disagree," says his mother. "People complain that we treat animals like objects, but in fact we treat them like prisoners of war. Do you know that when zoos were first opened to the public, the keepers had to protect the animals against attacks by spectators? The spectators felt the animals were there to be insulted and abused, like prisoners in a triumph. We had a war once against the animals, which we called hunting, though in fact war and hunting are the same thing (Aristotle saw it clearly).[1] That war went on for millions of years. We won it definitively only a few hundred years ago, when we invented guns. It is only since victory became absolute that we have been able to afford to cultivate compassion. But our compassion is very thinly spread. Beneath it is a more primitive attitude. The prisoner of war does not belong to our tribe. We can do what we want with him. We can sacrifice him to our gods. We can cut his throat, tear out his heart, throw him on the fire. There are no laws when it comes to prisoners of war."

"And that is what you want to cure humankind of?"

"John, I don't know what I want to do. I just don't want to sit silent."

"Very well. But generally one doesn't kill prisoners of war. One turns them into slaves."

"Well, that's what our captive herds are: slave populations. Their work is to breed for us. Even their sex becomes a form of labor. We don't hate them because they are not worth hating any more. We regard them, as you say, with contempt.

"However, there are still animals we hate. Rats, for instance. Rats haven't surrendered. They fight back. They form themselves into underground units in our sewers. They aren't winning, but they aren't losing either. To say nothing of the insects and the microbia. They may beat us yet. They will certainly outlast us."

The final session of his mother's visit is to take the form of a debate. Her opponent will be the large, blond man from yesterday evening's dinner, who turns out to be Thomas O'Hearne, professor of philosophy at Appleton.

It has been agreed that O'Hearne will have three opportunities to present positions, and his mother three opportunities to reply. Since O'Hearne has had the courtesy to send her a précis beforehand, she knows, broadly speaking, what he will be saying.

"My first reservation about the animal-rights movement," O'Hearne begins, "is that by failing to recognize its historical nature, it runs the risk of becoming, like the human-rights movement, yet another Western crusade against the practices of the rest of the world, claiming universality for what are simply its own standards." He proceeds to give a brief outline of the rise of animal-protection societies in Britain and America in the nineteenth century.

"When it comes to human rights," he continues, "other cultures and other religious traditions quite properly reply that they have their own norms and see no reason why they should have to adopt those of the West. Similarly, they say, they have their own norms for the treatment of animals and see no reason to adopt ours – particularly when ours are of such recent invention.

"In yesterday's presentation our lecturer was very hard on Descartes. But Descartes did not invent the idea that animals belong to a different order from humankind: he merely formalized it in a new way. The notion that we have an obligation to animals themselves to treat them compassionately – as opposed to an obligation to ourselves to do so – is very recent, very Western, and even very Anglo-Saxon. As long as we insist that we have access to an ethical universal to which other traditions are blind, and try to impose it on them by means of propaganda or even economic pressure, we are going to meet with resistance, and that resistance will be justified."

It is his mother's turn.

"The concerns you express are substantial, Professor O'Hearne, and I am not sure I can give them a substantial answer. You are correct, of course, about the history. Kindness to animals has become a social norm only recently, in the last hundred and fifty or two hundred years, and in only part of the world. You are correct too to link this history to the history of human rights, since concern for animals is, historically speaking, an offshoot of broader philanthropic concerns, for the lot of slaves and of children, among others.[2]

"However, kindness to animals – and here I use the word *kindness* in its full sense, as an acceptance that we are all of one kind, one nature – has been more widespread than you imply. Pet keeping, for instance, is by no means a Western fad: the first travel-

ers to South America encountered settle-
ments where human beings and animals
lived higgledy-piggledy together. And of
course children all over the world consort
quite naturally with animals. They don't see
any dividing line. That is something they
have to be taught, just as they have to be
taught it is all right to kill and eat them.

"Getting back to Descartes, I would only
want to say that the discontinuity he saw between animals and human beings was the
result of incomplete information. The science of Descartes's day had no acquain-
tance with the great apes or with higher
marine mammals, and thus little cause to
question the assumption that animals cannot think. And of course it had no access to
the fossil record that would reveal a graded
continuum of anthropoid creatures stretching from the higher primates to *Homo sapiens* — anthropoids, one must point out, who
were exterminated by man in the course of
his rise to power.[3]

"While I concede your main point about
Western cultural arrogance, I do think it is

appropriate that those who pioneered the industrialization of animal lives and the commodification of animal flesh should be at the forefront of trying to atone for it."

O'Hearne presents his second thesis. "In my reading of the scientific literature," he says, "efforts to show that animals can think strategically, hold general concepts, or communicate symbolically, have had very limited success. The best performance the higher apes can put up is no better than that of a speech-impaired human being with severe mental retardation. If so, are not animals, even the higher animals, properly thought of as belonging to another legal and ethical realm entirely, rather than being placed in this depressing human subcategory? Isn't there a certain wisdom in the traditional view that says that animals cannot enjoy legal rights because they are not persons, even potential persons, as fetuses are? In working out rules for our dealings with animals, does it not make more sense for such rules to apply to us and to our treatment of them, as at present, rather than being predicated upon rights which animals cannot claim or enforce or even understand?"[4]

His mother's turn. "To respond adequately, Professor O'Hearne, would take more time than I have, since I would first want to interrogate the whole question of rights and how we come to possess them. So let me just make one observation: that the program of scientific experimentation that leads you to conclude that animals are imbeciles is profoundly anthropocentric. It values being able to find your way out of a sterile maze, ignoring the fact that if the researcher who designed the maze were to be parachuted into the jungles of Borneo, he or she would be dead of starvation in a week. In fact I would go further. If I as a human being were told that the standards by which animals are being measured in these experiments are human standards, I would be insulted. It is the experiments themselves that are imbecile. The behaviorists who design them claim that we understand only by a process of creating abstract models and then testing those models against reality. What nonsense. We understand by immersing ourselves and our intelligence in complexity. There is something self-stultified in the way in which scientific behaviorism recoils from the complexity of life.[5]

"As for animals being too dumb and stupid to speak for themselves, consider the following sequence of events. When Albert Camus was a young boy in Algeria, his grandmother told him to bring her one of the hens from the cage in their backyard. He obeyed, then watched her cut off its head with a kitchen knife, catching its blood in a bowl so that the floor would not be dirtied.

"The death-cry of that hen imprinted itself on the boy's memory so hauntingly that in 1958 he wrote an impassioned attack on the guillotine. As a result, in part, of that polemic, capital punishment was abolished in France. Who is to say, then, that the hen did not speak?"[6]

O'Hearne. "I make the following statement with due deliberation, mindful of the historical associations it may evoke. I do not believe that life is as important to animals as it is to us. There is certainly in animals an instinctive struggle against death, which they share with us. But they do not *understand* death as we do, or rather, as we fail to do. There is, in the human mind, a collapse of the imagination before death, and that collapse of the imagination – graphically evoked in yesterday's lecture – is the basis of our fear of death. That fear does not and cannot exist in animals, since the effort to comprehend extinction, and the failure to do so, the failure to master it, have simply not taken place.

"For that reason, I want to suggest, dying is, for an animal, just something that happens, something against which there may be a revolt of the organism but not a revolt of the soul. And the lower down the scale of evolution one goes, the truer this is. To an insect, death is the breakdown of systems that keep the physical organism functioning, and nothing more.

"To animals, death is continuous with life. It is only among certain very imaginative human beings that one encounters a horror of dying so acute that they then project it onto other beings, including animals. Animals live, and then they die: that is all. Thus to equate a butcher who slaughters a chicken with an executioner who kills a human being is a grave mistake. The events are not comparable. They are not of the same scale, they are not on the same scale.

"That leaves us with the question of cruelty. It is licit to kill animals, I would say, because their lives are not as important to them as our lives are to us; the old-fashioned way of saying this is that animals do not have immortal souls. Gratuitous cruelty, on the other hand, I would regard as illicit. Therefore it is quite appropriate that we should agitate for the humane treatment of animals, even and particularly in slaughterhouses. This has for a long time been a goal of animal welfare organizations, and I salute them for it.

"My very last point concerns what I see as the troublingly abstract nature of the concern for animals in the animal-rights movement. I want to apologize in advance to our lecturer for the seeming harshness of what I am about to say, but I believe it needs to be said.

"Of the many varieties of animal-lover I see around me, let me isolate two. On the one hand, hunters, people who value animals at a very elementary, unreflective level; who spend hours watching them and tracking them; and who, after they have killed them, get pleasure from the taste of their flesh. On the other hand, people who have little contact with animals, or at least with those species they are concerned to protect, like poultry and livestock, yet want all animals to lead – in an economic vacuum – a utopian life in which everyone is miraculously fed and no one preys on anyone else.

"Of the two, which, I ask, loves animals more?

"It is because agitation for animal rights, including the right to life, is so abstract that I find it unconvincing and, finally, idle. Its proponents talk a great deal about our community with animals, but how do they actually live that community? Thomas Aquinas says that friendship between human beings and animals is impossible, and I tend to agree.[7] You can be friends neither with a Martian nor with a bat, for the simple reason that you have too little in common with them. We may certainly *wish* for there to be community with animals, but that is not the same thing as living in community with them. It is just a piece of prelapsarian wistfulness."

His mother's turn again, her last turn.

"Anyone who says that life matters less to animals than it does to us has not held in his hands an animal fighting for its life. The whole of the being of the animal is thrown into that fight, without reserve. When you say that the fight lacks a dimension of intellectual or imaginative horror, I agree. It is not the mode of being of animals to have an intellectual horror: their whole being is in the living flesh.

"If I do not convince you, that is because my words, here, lack the power to bring home to you the wholeness, the unabstracted, unintellectual nature, of that animal being. That is why I urge you to read the poets who return the living, electric being to language; and if the poets do not move you, I urge you to walk, flank to flank, beside the beast that is prodded down the chute to his executioner.

"You say that death does not matter to an animal because the animal does not understand death. I am reminded of one of the academic philosophers I read in preparing for yesterday's lecture. It was a depressing experience. It awoke in me a quite Swiftian response. If this is the best that human philosophy can offer, I said to myself, I would rather go and live among horses.

"Can we, asked this philosopher, strictly speaking, say that the veal calf misses its mother? Does the veal calf have enough of a grasp of the significance of the mother-relation, does the veal calf have enough of a grasp of the meaning of maternal absence, does the veal calf, finally, know enough about missing to know that the feeling it has is the feeling of missing?[8]

"A calf who has not mastered the concepts of presence and absence, of self and others – so goes the argument – cannot, strictly speaking, be said to miss anything. In order to, strictly speaking, miss anything, it would first have to take a course in philosophy. What sort of philosophy is this? Throw it out, I say. What good do its piddling distinctions do?

"To me, a philosopher who says that the distinction between human and nonhuman depends on whether you have a white or a black skin, and a philosopher who says that the distinction between human and nonhuman depends on whether or not you know the difference between a subject and a predicate, are more alike than they are unlike.

"Usually I am wary of exclusionary gestures. I know of one prominent philosopher who states that he is simply not prepared to philosophize about animals with people who eat meat. I am not sure I would go as far as that – frankly, I have not the courage – but I must say I would not fall over myself to meet the gentleman whose book I just have been citing. Specifically, I would not fall over myself to break bread with him.

"Would I be prepared to discuss ideas with him? That really is the crucial question. Discussion is possible only when there is common ground. When opponents are at loggerheads, we say: 'Let them reason together, and by reasoning clarify what their differences are, and thus inch closer. They may seem to share nothing else, but at least they share reason.'

"On the present occasion, however, I am not sure I want to concede that I share reason with my opponent. Not when reason is what underpins the whole long philosophical tradition to which he belongs, stretching back to Descartes and beyond Descartes through Aquinas and Augustine to the Stoics and Aristotle. If the last common ground that I have with him is reason, and if reason is what sets me apart from the veal calf, then thank you but no thank you, I'll talk to someone else."

That is the note on which Dean Arendt

has to bring the proceedings to a close: acri-
mony, hostility, bitterness. He, John
Bernard, is sure that is not what Arendt or
his committee wanted. Well, they should
have asked him before they invited his
mother. He could have told them.

It is past midnight, he and Norma are in
bed, he is exhausted, at six he will have to
get up to drive his mother to the airport. But
Norma is in a fury and will not give up. "It's
nothing but food-faddism, and food-faddism is always an exercise in power. I have
no patience when she arrives here and begins trying to get people, particularly the
children, to change their eating habits. And
now these absurd public lectures! She is trying to extend her inhibiting power over the
whole community!"

He wants to sleep, but he cannot utterly
betray his mother. "She's perfectly sincere," he murmurs.

"It has nothing to do with sincerity. She
has no self-insight at all. It is because she

has so little insight into her motives that she seems sincere. Mad people are sincere."

With a sigh he enters the fray. "I don't see any difference," he says, "between her revulsion from eating meat and my own revulsion from eating snails or locusts. I have no insight into my motives and I couldn't care less. I just find it disgusting."

Norma snorts. "You don't give public lectures producing pseudophilosophical arguments for not eating snails. You don't try to turn a private fad into a public taboo."

"Perhaps. But why not try to see her as a preacher, a social reformer, rather than as an eccentric trying to foist her preferences on to other people?"

"You are welcome to see her as a preacher. But take a look at all the other preachers and their crazy schemes for dividing mankind up into the saved and the damned. Is that the kind of company you want your mother to keep? Elizabeth Costello and her Second Ark, with her dogs and cats and wolves, none of whom, of course, has ever been guilty of the sin of eating flesh, to say nothing of the malaria virus and the rabies virus and the HI virus, which she will want to save so that she can restock her Brave New World."

"Norma, you're ranting."

"I'm not ranting. I would have more respect for her if she didn't try to undermine me behind my back, with her stories to the children about the poor little veal calves and what the bad men do to them. I'm tired of having them pick at their food and ask, 'Mom, is this veal?' when it's chicken or tuna-fish. It's nothing but a power-game. Her great hero Franz Kafka played the same game with his family. He refused to eat this, he refused to eat that, he would rather starve, he said. Soon everyone was feeling guilty about eating in front of him, and he could sit back feeling virtuous. It's a sick game, and I'm not having the children play it against me."[9]

"A few hours and she'll be gone, then we can return to normal."

"Good. Say goodbye to her from me. I'm not getting up early."

Seven o'clock, the sun just rising, and he
and his mother are on their way to the airport.

"I'm sorry about Norma," he says. "She
has been under a lot of strain. I don't think
she is in a position to sympathize. Perhaps
one could say the same for me. It's been
such a short visit, I haven't had time to make
sense of why you have become so intense
about the animal business."

She watches the wipers wagging back
and forth. "A better explanation," she says,
"is that I have not told you why, or dare not
tell you. When I think of the words, they
seem so outrageous that they are best spoken into a pillow or into a hole in the
ground, like King Midas."

"I don't follow. What is it you can't say?"

"It's that I no longer know where I am. I
seem to move around perfectly easily
among people, to have perfectly normal relations with them. Is it possible, I ask myself, that all of them are participants in a

crime of stupefying proportions? Am I fantasizing it all? I must be mad! Yet every day I see the evidences. The very people I suspect produce the evidence, exhibit it, offer it to me. Corpses. Fragments of corpses that they have bought for money.

"It is as if I were to visit friends, and to make some polite remark about the lamp in their living room, and they were to say, 'Yes, it's nice, isn't it? Polish-Jewish skin it's made of, we find that's best, the skins of young Polish-Jewish virgins.' And then I go to the bathroom and the soap-wrapper says, 'Treblinka – 100% human stearate.' Am I dreaming, I say to myself? What kind of house is this?

"Yet I'm not dreaming. I look into your eyes, into Norma's, into the children's, and I see only kindness, human-kindness. Calm down, I tell myself, you are making a mountain out of a molehill. This is life. Everyone else comes to terms with it, why can't you? *Why can't you?*"

She turns on him a tearful face. What does she want, he thinks? Does she want me to answer her question for her?

They are not yet on the expressway. He pulls the car over, switches off the engine, takes his mother in his arms. He inhales the smell of cold cream, of old flesh. "There, there," he whispers in her ear. "There, there. It will soon be over."

NOTES

1   Aristotle: "The art of war is a natural art of acquisition, for the art of acquisition includes hunting, an art which we ought to practise against wild beasts, and against men who, though intended by nature to be governed, will not submit; for war of such a kind is naturally just." *Politics* 1.8, in Regan and Singer, *Animal Rights*, 110.

2   See James Turner, *Reckoning with the Beast* (Baltimore: Johns Hopkins University Press, 1980), chap. 1.

3   See Mary Midgley, "Persons and Non-Persons," in *In Defence of Animals*, ed. Peter Singer (Oxford: Blackwell, 1985), 59; Rosemary Rodd, *Biology, Ethics, and Animals* (Oxford: Clarendon Press, 1990), 37.

4   Cf. Bernard Williams: "Before one gets to the question of how animals should be treated, there is the fundamental point that this is the only question there can be: how they should be treated. The choice can only be whether

animals benefit from our practices or are harmed by them." Quoted in Michael P. T. Leahy, *Against Liberation* (London and New York: Routledge, 1991), 208.

5   For a critique of behaviorism in the political context of its times, see Bernard E. Rollin, *The Unheeded Cry* (Oxford: Oxford University Press, 1990), 100–103. On the behaviorist taboo on considering the subjective mental states of animals, see Donald R. Griffin, *Animal Minds* (Chicago: University of Chicago Press, 1992), 6–7. Griffin calls the taboo "a serious impediment to scientific investigation" but suggests that in practice investigators do not adhere to it (6, 120).

6   Albert Camus, *The First Man*, trans. David Hapgood (London: Hamish Hamilton, 1995), 181–83; Réflexions sur la guillotine, in *Essais*, ed. R. Quilliot and L. Faucon (Paris: Gallimard, 1965), 1019–64.

7   *Summa* 2.65.3, quoted in Regan and Singer, *Animal Rights*, 120.

8   Leahy, *Against Liberation*, 218. Leahy elsewhere argues against a ban on the slaughtering of animals on the grounds that (a) it would bring about unemployment among abattoir workers, (b) it would entail an uncomfortable adjustment to our diet, and (c) the countryside would be less attractive without its customary flocks and herds fattening themselves as they wait to die (214).

9   "What [Kafka] required was a regimen of eccentric food habits that were at odds with the 'normal' dinner table habits of his family …. Kafka's form of anorexia – not to lose weight but to use food ritualistically as a form of superior statement – was a way of bridging the gap between himself and his family, while at the same time insisting on his uniqueness, his superiority, his sense of rejection." Karl, *Franz Kafka*, 188.